A
atheneum

ATHENEUM BOOKS FOR YOUNG READERS
An imprint of Simon & Schuster Children's Publishing Division
1230 Avenue of the Americas, New York, New York 10020
Text copyright © 2013 by Ann Bonwill
Illustrations copyright © 2013 by Simon Rickerty
First published in Great Britain in 2013 by Oxford University Press
Photograph on page 4 copyright © 2013 by Stephanie Angue/
Shutterstock.com
All rights reserved, including the right of reproduction in whole or
in part in any form.
ATHENEUM BOOKS FOR YOUNG READERS is a registered trademark of
Simon & Schuster, Inc.
Atheneum logo is a trademark of Simon & Schuster, Inc.
For information about special discounts for bulk purchases, please
contact Simon & Schuster Special Sales at 1-866-506-1949 or
business@simonandschuster.com.
The Simon & Schuster Speakers Bureau can bring authors to your
live event. For more information or to book an event, contact the
Simon & Schuster Speakers Bureau at 1-866-248-3049 or visit our
website at www.simonspeakers.com.
Book design by Sonia Chaghatzbanian
The text for this book is set in VAG Rounded, Family Dog, Skizzors,
and Giggles BTN.
The illustrations for this book are rendered digitally.
Manufactured in China
1112 OUP
First U.S. Edition 2013
2 4 6 8 10 9 7 5 3 1
CIP data for this book is available from the Library of Congress.
ISBN 978-1-4424-8053-7

I Am Not a Copycat!

written by
Ann Bonwill

illustrated by
Simon Rickerty

Atheneum Books for Young Readers • New York London Toronto Sydney New Delhi

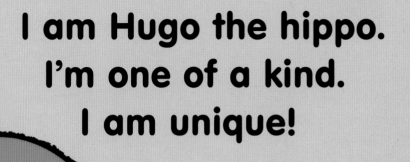

I am Hugo the hippo.
I'm one of a kind.
I am unique!

What are we doing?

I was being unique. Until YOU came along, Bella.

Oh, sorry. That's quite a hat, by the way.

Thank you! But as I was saying, before I was so rudely interrupted . . .

I'm practicing moves for my water ballet.

I don't know another hippo who can . . .

Touch his toes . . .

Nope, can't think of anyone.
Great goggles!

Or even do a split!

It's true. There's no one like you: You are unique. Right down to your flippers.

I would be, except that **YOU** keep copying me!

Wow! Nice floaties.
Where are we going?

And besides, I want to be unique too. Just like you.

Aargh!

Swimming Pool

But only I can do a triple backflip.

Right. Only you.

Bella, will you **stop** being a copycat!

I am not a copycat. I am a bird.

**Bravo! says another hippo.
May I take your photo?
You two are amazing
synchronized swimmers!**

I agRee, says anotheR
biRd. YouR teaM is
tRuLy uNique!

See, Hugo,
I wasn't
ruining
your ballet.
I was
making
it better!

Yes, I suppose you were. Thanks, Bella. I think we're famous!

This way for ice cream

How about some ice cream to celebrate?

I'll have strawberry swirl
with vanilla wafers and
minty sprinkles.

And I'll have
exactly the same!

You're right, Bella, it is
lots of fun to be alike.

I guess so, sometimes,
but maybe this time
I'll change mine to...

...double
chocolate chip.